This book
belongs to

Jack Fergason

is cool and awsom

Munsch More!

A Robert Munsch Collection

Illustrated by

Michael Martchenko

Alan and Lea Daniel

and

Eugenie Fernandes

Scholastic Canada Ltd.

New York Toronto London Auckland Sydney

Mexico City New Delhi Hong Kong Buenos Aires

Library and Archives Canada Cataloguing in Publication
Munsch, Robert N., 1945-
Munsch more / Robert Munsch; illustrated by Michael Martchenko... [et al.].

Contents: Alligator baby – Andrew's loose tooth – Get out of bed! – Ribbon rescue – Mmm, cookies – Deep snow.
ISBN 0-439-96135-1

1. Children's stories, Canadian (English) I. Martchenko, Michael II. Title.

PS8576.U575M85 2004 jC813'.54 C2004-900759-9

6 5 4 3 Printed in Singapore 04 05 06 07

Contents

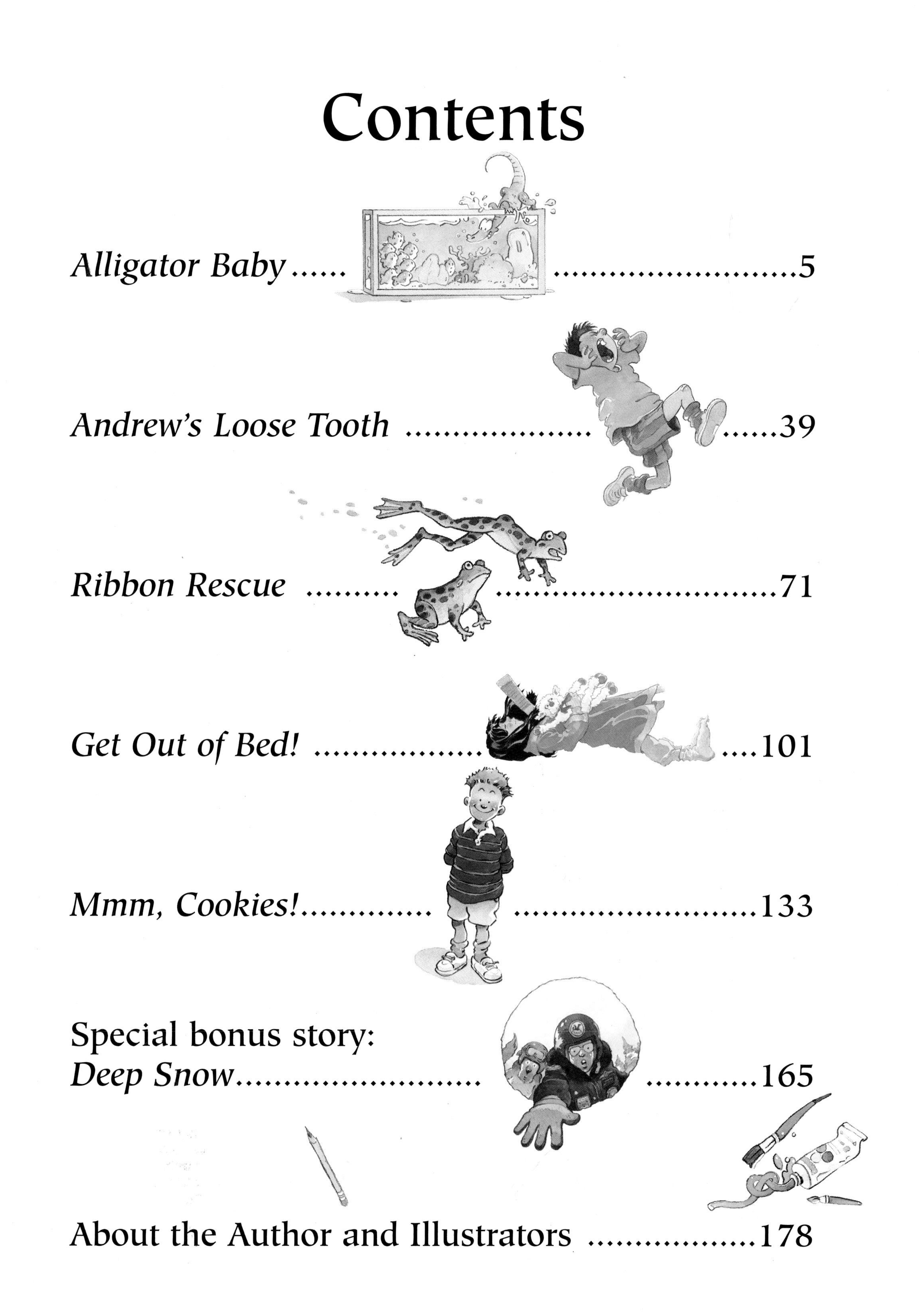

Alligator Baby 5

Andrew's Loose Tooth 39

Ribbon Rescue 71

Get Out of Bed! 101

Mmm, Cookies! 133

Special bonus story:
Deep Snow 165

About the Author and Illustrators 178

To Kristen Bocking,
Guelph, Ontario.
—R.M.

Alligator Baby

by Robert Munsch

illustrated by Michael Martchenko

One night Kristen's mother woke up and yelled, "A baby! A baby! I'm having a baby!"

Kristen's father jumped up, zoomed around the room, got dressed, and grabbed Kristen's mother by the hand. They ran downstairs to the car and drove off really fast.

Varoooooooooommmm.

Unfortunately, they got lost. They didn't go to the hospital, they went to the *zoo*. But it was okay. Kristen's mother had a lovely baby. Then they drove home and knocked on their front door: *blam, blam, blam, blam, blam.*

Kristen opened the door and there was her mother, holding something all wrapped up.

"Kristen," she said, "would you like to see your new baby brother?"

"Oh, yes," said Kristen.

So Kristen lifted up the bottom of the blanket. She saw a long green tail and said, "That's not a people tail."

Kristen lifted up the middle of the blanket, saw a green claw, and said, "That's not a people claw."

Kristen lifted up the top of the blanket, saw a long green face with lots of teeth, and said, "That's not a people face! That is *not* my baby brother!"

"Now, Kristen," said her mother, "don't be jealous."

Just then the baby reached up and bit Kristen's mother on the nose. She yelled, *"Aaaaaahhhhaaaaa!"*

Then the baby reached up and bit her father on the nose. He yelled, *"Aaaaaahhhhaaaaa!"*

"That's not a people baby," said Kristen. "That's an alligator baby."

"Goodness," said her mother. "We've got the wrong baby!"

So Kristen put the alligator baby into the fish tank, and her mother and father drove back to the zoo. They came back in an hour and knocked on the door: *blam, blam, blam, blam, blam.*

Kristen opened the door and her mother said, "Would you like to see your new baby brother?"

"Oh, yes," said Kristen.

Kristen lifted up the bottom of the blanket, saw a fishy tail, and said, "That's not a people tail."

Kristen lifted up the middle of the blanket, saw a flipper, and said, "That's not a people flipper."

Kristen lifted up the top of the blanket, saw a face with whiskers, and said, "That's not a people face. That is *not* my baby brother!"

"Now, Kristen," said her mother, "don't be jealous."

Just then the baby reached up with its flipper and flapped her father's face: *wap, wap, wap, wap, wap, wap, wap.*

He yelled, *"Aaaaaahhhhaaaaa!* It's a seal baby! We've got the wrong baby."

So Kristen put the seal baby in the bathtub, and her mother and father drove back to the zoo.

They came back in an hour and knocked on the door: *blam, blam, blam, blam, blam.* They said, "Kristen, would you like to see your new baby brother?"

"Oh, yes," said Kristen.

She lifted up the bottom of the blanket, saw a very hairy leg, and said, "That's not a people leg."

She lifted up the middle of the blanket, saw a very hairy arm, and said, "That's not a people arm."

She lifted up the top of the blanket, saw a very hairy face, and said, "That's not a people face. That is *not* my baby brother!"

"Now, Kristen," said her mother, "don't be jealous."

Then the baby reached up with its feet and grabbed her mother's ear and her father's ear, and they both yelled, "*Aaaaaahhhhaaaaa!* It's a gorilla baby! We've got the wrong baby!"

"Let me do it," said Kristen.

So her mother and father put the gorilla baby on the chandelier in the living room, and Kristen went off to the zoo on her bicycle.

First Kristen looked in the snake cage. No people babies.

Then Kristen looked in the wombat cage. No people babies.

Then Kristen looked in the elephant cage. No people babies.

Then she stopped and listened. From far away she heard, *"Waaa, waaa, waaa, waaa, waaa."*

"That's more like it!" said Kristen. She followed the sound. It was coming from the gorilla cage.

Kristen looked at the mommy gorilla and said, “Give me my baby brother.” The gorilla jumped away and wouldn’t give the baby back at all.

Then the people baby reached up and bit the gorilla on the nose, and the gorilla yelled, "*Aaaaaahhhhaaaaa!*" and handed the baby to Kristen.

Kristen jumped on her bicycle and pedalled home.

Kristen knocked on the door: *blam, blam, blam, blam, blam.* When her parents opened it, she said, "Would you like to see your new baby?"

Kristen's mother lifted up the bottom of the blanket, and said, "Look, people legs."

She lifted up the middle of the blanket, and said, "Look, people hands."

She lifted up the top of the blanket, and said, "Look, a people face."

Kristen's mother picked up the baby and gave it a big hug. Her father took the baby and gave it a big hug. And her mother said, "Kristen, Kristen. You got the baby back. Good for you."

"But what are we going to do with all these other babies?" yelled Kristen's father. "There is a seal baby in the bathtub and an alligator baby in the fish tank and a gorilla baby hanging from the chandelier! We should take them back to the zoo."

But Kristen looked out the window and said . . .

"I don't think we'll have to do anything at all."

And everything was okay . . .
until Kristen's mother had twins.

About Alligator Baby

In 1979, some friends of mine were having a birthday party for their daughter, Kristen. I had been Kristen's teacher at nursery school, and I volunteered to tell stories at her party. Since Kristen's mom was going to have a baby, I made up a new story about how her mom and dad made a mistake, went to the zoo instead of the hospital, and brought home a baby alligator! Kristen liked the story so much that she wrote it all down and drew some pictures to make her own little book.

Years later, when I wanted to make the story into a book, I tracked her down and asked if she still wanted to be the kid in the book. Kristen said that she would be delighted. Kristen likes my book, but she still thinks that her own illustrated version is better.

— R.M.

For Andrew Munsch,
Guelph, Ontario.
–R.M.

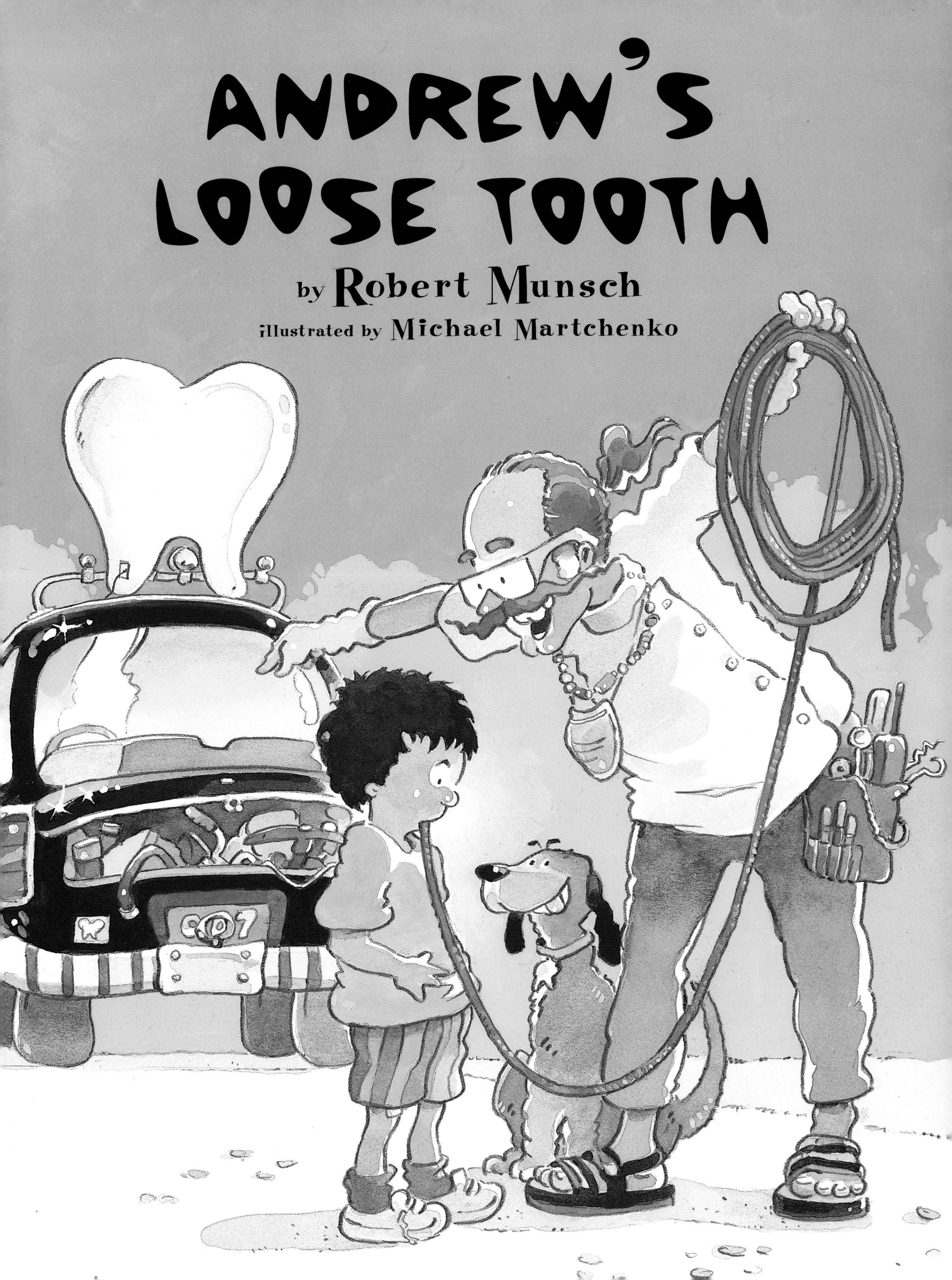
ANDREW'S LOOSE TOOTH
by Robert Munsch
illustrated by Michael Martchenko

When Andrew came downstairs, there were three big red apples in the middle of the table. And even though he had a loose tooth, he decided to eat an apple.

So he reached out,
picked up an apple,
shined it on his shirt,
took a bite,
and yelled, "YEEE-OW!
Mommy, Mommy! Do something about this tooth. It hurts so much I can't even eat my apple."

Andrew's mother opened up his mouth and looked inside.

"Ooh, ooh, ooh!" she said. "It's a loose tooth! I know what to do."

She took hold of the tooth with both hands and pulled as hard as she could. But the tooth did not come out.

"Oh, Andrew," she said, "I just can't get that tooth out. Why don't you try another apple? That might make your tooth come out."

So Andrew reached out,
picked up an apple,
shined it on his shirt,
took a bite,
and yelled, "YEEE-OW!
Daddy, Daddy! Do something about this tooth. It hurts so much I can't even eat my apple."

So Andrew's father opened up his mouth and looked inside.

"Ooh, ooh, ooh!" he said. "It's a loose tooth! I know what to do."

He got a big pair of pliers and took hold of Andrew's tooth. Then he put his foot on Andrew's nose and pulled as hard as he could. But the tooth did not come out.

"Oh, Andrew," he said, "this tooth is stuck. Why don't you try another apple? That will make your tooth come out."

So Andrew reached out,
picked up an apple,
shined it on his shirt,
took a bite,
and yelled, "**YEEE-OW!**
Mommy, Daddy, Mommy, Daddy! Do something about this tooth. It hurts so much I can't even eat my apple."

So they called a dentist.

The dentist came in a shiny black car. He opened up Andrew's mouth, looked inside and said, "Ooh, ooh, ooh! It's a loose tooth! I know what to do."

555-TOOTH
007

He got a big, long rope and he tied one end to Andrew's tooth.

Andrew said, "I know what you're going to do! I know what you're going to do! You're going to tie the end of the rope to the door and then you're going to slam the door!"

"NO!" said the dentist. "I'm going to tie it to my car."

He tied the other end of the rope to his car and drove away as fast as he could. When he got to the end of the rope, his whole car fell apart. The dentist stood there holding just the steering wheel.

Then Andrew's mother and his father and the dentist all said, "Andrew, Andrew. That tooth will not come out. You just can't eat your breakfast."

Andrew sat out in the front yard looking very sad. His best friend, Louis, came along and said, "Andrew, what's the matter?"

"Oh," said Andrew, "my mother can't get this tooth out. My father can't get this tooth out. The dentist can't get this tooth out. And I can't eat my breakfast."

"Ooh, ooh, ooh!" said Louis. "I know what to do."

Louis went into Andrew's house and called the Tooth Fairy on the phone. The Tooth Fairy roared up right away on a large motorcycle.

Andrew looked at the Tooth Fairy and said, "If you think you are going to use that motorcycle to pull out my tooth, you are nuts."

"What do you think I am?" said the Tooth Fairy. "A dentist?"

She pulled Andrew's tooth with one hand and the tooth did not come out.

She pulled Andrew's tooth with two hands and the tooth did not come out.

She got a large hammer off her motorcycle and clanged Andrew's loose tooth. The hammer broke in two pieces, and the tooth still did not come out.

"Incredible," said the Tooth Fairy. "This is the first tooth ever that I can't pull out. I guess you just can't eat your breakfast!"

"Hold it," said Louis, "I have an idea."

Louis went into Andrew's house and got a pepper shaker. Then he pushed back Andrew's head and sprinkled pepper up Andrew's nose.

Andrew went,

"Ah, Ahhh,

Ah, Ahhhh,

AHHHHH-CHOO!"

. . . and sneezed that tooth all the way across town.

But the Tooth Fairy still got her tooth.

About Andrew's Loose Tooth

In 1982, I was on a tour of Saskatchewan for the Canadian Children's Book Centre. I was visiting three towns a day and telling stories in schools and libraries. One of the towns was Fort Qu'Appelle, which is in the middle of an enormous valley that cuts through the mostly flat prairie. There, I ended up telling stories to a whole gym full of kids. Grade 2 was in the front and lots of the kids were missing teeth. I thought, "I bet these kids would like a tooth story," so I made one up. It was not very good, but the kids liked it because they all had loose teeth.

I kept telling it for years and years and the story got good without me noticing it! Kids started asking, "When are you going to make the tooth story into a book?" Finally, I decided to really listen to myself while I told the story and I was happy to see that the not-very-good tooth story had turned into a really-very-good tooth story, in only ten years.

I decided to use my son, Andrew, in the book. Louis, a friend of Andrew's, is also in the book. Louis is Greek and said it was OK to use him in the story, but only if I put a Greek flag on his shirt.

— R.M.

For Jillian DeLaronde,
Kahnawake, Quebec.
–R.M.

For Robyn, Julia,
Alexandra and Katherine.
–E.F.

Ribbon Rescue

by Robert Munsch
illustrated by
Eugenie Fernandes

As soon as her grandmother finished making the ribbon dress, Jillian put it on and ran out into the front yard.

A man came running down the road. He was dressed in fancy clothes and he was yelling:

"I'm late, I'm lost!
I'm late, I'm lost!
I'm going to miss my own wedding."

"Wait," said Jillian. "Let me fix your shoes." She tore two ribbons off her dress, laced the man's shoes with them, and tied them into big bows.

The man said, "Thanks. I may be late, but I'll look fine."

"Well," said Jillian, "why don't you take my brother Lewis's skateboard. He is grown up and doesn't use it anymore. Just keep your eye on the church steeple and you will get there."

"Thank you," said the man. "I'll bring it back as soon as the wedding is over."

Then a lady in a fancy white dress came running by. She was yelling:

"I'm late, I'm lost!

I'm late, I'm lost!

I'm going to miss my own wedding."

"Well," said Jillian, "at least I can fix your hair."

Jillian reached up and tore eight ribbons off her dress: one, two, three, four, five, six, seven, eight. Then the lady bent down and Jillian fixed her hair into four enormous ponytails.

"And now," said Jillian, "take my mother's bicycle. She is grown up and doesn't use it very much. Just keep heading for the church steeple and you will be there in no time."

"Oh, thank you," said the lady. "I might be late, but at least I will look okay." She gave Jillian a hug and rode away on the bicycle.

Then a family came running down the road yelling:

"We're late. We're lost!

We're late. We're lost!

We're going to miss the wedding.

We haven't even had time to wrap the present."

"Well," said Jillian, "I can wrap your present." And she wrapped the present with five ribbons from her dress.

The family said, “Oh, thank you. Thank you. Thank you. Thank you. We may be late, but we will have a lovely present.”

“And now,” said Jillian, “take Lindsay’s wagon and Hayley’s scooter. They are sort of grown up and don’t use them very much. Just keep heading for the church steeple and you will not get lost.”

They all gave Jillian a hug and raced off.

Then a man came down the road yelling,

"I'm late. I'm lost!

I'm late. I'm lost!

I'm going to miss the wedding."

Suddenly he stopped and said, "Oh, NO! It's lost!"

"What's lost?" said Jillian.

"The ring! The wedding ring!" said the man. "I've lost the ring."

"I'll help you find it," said Jillian.

She crawled around and got quite dirty, but after a while she found the ring in a mud puddle.

"Look," said Jillian, "you might lose it again. Let me help you."

She tied the ring to the man's finger with a ribbon.

"And now," said Jillian, "take Jeremy's skates. He is grown up and doesn't use them very much. Just keep heading for the church steeple."

"Thank you," said the man. "I may be late, but at least I'll have the ring."

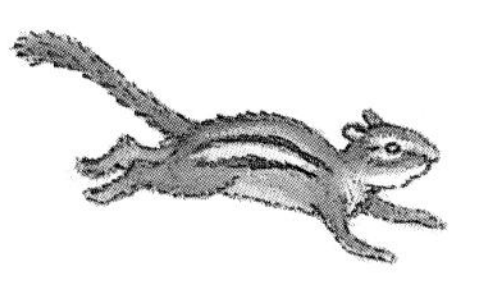

Then Jillian's mother came running out of the house, yelling, "Jillian, we're late for a wedding and you're a mess. What will your grandmother say?"

She grabbed Jillian's hand and they ran down the road.

But when they got to the church the man at the door said to Jillian, "What a mess! You can't come in here dressed like that!"

"But, but . . . ," said her mother.

"That's okay," said Jillian. "I will sit on the stairs and wait for you."

Then the bride and groom walked around the side of the church and saw Jillian sitting on the stairs.

"Oh," said the groom. "Don't my shoes look great?"

"Oh," said the bride. "Isn't my hair wonderful?"

"Yes," said Jillian. "Your shoes are great and your hair is wonderful and I hope you have a wonderful wedding."

"Aren't you coming in?" said the groom.

"No," said Jillian, "I tore off all my ribbons to fix hair, lace shoes, wrap a present, and tie a ring. Now my dress is a mess and I can't come in."

"Hhhhuuummm," said the groom. "I think we need a flower girl."

"Hhhhuuummm," said the bride. "Yes, we definitely need a flower girl."

So they picked a bunch of wildflowers from the grass and Jillian walked into the church in front of everybody else.

And even though her dress was all dirty and full of holes, everyone said she was the prettiest kid there.

About Ribbon Rescue

In 1993, I was in Montreal making a video. A boy and a girl came very early to be in the audience, and they were standing in the middle of this huge TV studio looking lost. I decided to tell them stories. We went off into a corner and I spent half an hour making up new stories. One of them was about a ribbon dress that the little girl was wearing. I had never seen a ribbon dress before.

The next day I decided that the ribbon story was too good to forget and I wrote it down, but I did not even remember the girl's name. The people at the TV studio said that maybe she was from the Mohawk reserve at Kahnawake, across the river from Montreal. I found Jillian, and I also found out that there were lots of ribbon dresses at Kahnawake. To dress up really fancy, Mohawk girls wear ribbon dresses and Mohawk boys wear ribbon shirts. Years later, when I thought the story might become a book, I went to Kahnawake and visited Jillian and her family. I took lots of pictures, which Eugenie Fernandes used to help her illustrate the book. After *Ribbon Rescue* was published in 1999, I did a storytelling at Jillian's school. Lots of girls wore their ribbon dresses. In 2004, the whole story came out in a local Mohawk edition. In it Jillian is called "Teiohathe," which is her real Mohawk name.

– R.M.

For Amy Albrecht,
Tavistock, Ontario.
–R.M.

To Carolyn and David.
–A.D. and L.D.

Get Out Of Bed!

by **Robert Munsch**

illustrated by
Alan & Lea Daniel

In the middle of the night, when
everyone else was asleep, Amy went downstairs.
She watched
The Late Show,
The Late, Late Show,
The Late, Late, Late, Late Show
The Early, Early, Early, Early Show,
and finally went to bed because
she was feeling somewhat tired.

The next morning everyone came
to the breakfast table . . . except Amy.
"Where is Amy?" said her father.
"Where is Amy?" said her brother.
"Amy is asleep," said her mother.
"I have called her five times and she is
still asleep. What are we going to do?"
"No problem," said her brother.
"I can get her up."

Amy's brother ran up the stairs
and yelled as loudly
as he could: "**Aaaaaaammyyy!!!**"

Amy snored. **zzz-zzz-zzz-zzz-zzz**

"Be late for school," he said. "See if I care." And he ran back downstairs.

"Well, I know what to do," said Amy's father.

He walked up the stairs and said in his sternest father voice, **“Amy, if you don’t get out of this bed this instant, I am going to be very mad!”**

Amy snored. **ZZZ-ZZZ-ZZZ-ZZZ-ZZZ**

He went back downstairs and told Amy’s mother, “Your daughter will not get up.”

“Well, I have something that sometimes works,” she said.

She ran up the stairs,
stood Amy on her feet
and said very nicely,
"Amy, please wake up."

Amy fell over and
went to sleep on the floor.

zzz-zzz-zzz-zzz-zzz

Her mother ran back
downstairs and said,
"I can't get her up!
I can't get her up!"

"Oh no!" said her father.
"I have to go to work."

"Oh no!" said her brother.
"I have to go to school."

"I have to go to work, too,"
said her mother. "But what
are we going to do with Amy?"

"Let's take her to school in her bed,"
said her brother.

Amy's mother and father looked
at each other and said, "Good idea."

So they put Amy back in her bed and picked it up. Then they walked

out the front door,

down the street,

around the corner,

through the schoolyard,

and into the school.

They put the bed down in the back of the classroom and left.

Later that day, the principal came in and said, "What is going on here?"

"I don't know," said the teacher. "It's Amy. She will not get out of bed."

"No problem," said the principal.

She walked over and yelled at Amy as loud as she could:

"**WAKE UP!**"

Amy snored. ***zzz-ZZZ-ZZZ-ZZZ***

"I give up," said the principal.

So the teacher taught reading, and Amy didn't wake up.

The teacher taught arithmetic, and Amy didn't wake up.

They went to gym, and Amy didn't wake up.
They went out for recess, and Amy didn't wake up.

They had lunch, and Amy didn't wake up.
They had art, and Amy still didn't wake up.

Finally, it was time to go home.

"Call the mother. Call the father," yelled the principal. "Get this kid out of here."

So Amy's mother came from work, and her father came from work, and her brother came from school. They picked up Amy's bed, carried it home, and all had dinner . . . except Amy. Amy was asleep.

zzz-zzz-zzz-zzz-zzz

"If she never gets up," said her brother, "can I have her room?"

But the next morning Amy did get up. She ran downstairs and said, "Oh, I'm hungry. I haven't eaten in years!"

"Nice to see you," said her mother. "Did you have a nice sleep?"

"Wonderful," said Amy, "but I had strange dreams."

Then her mother went to work and her father went to work, and Amy and her brother went to school.

At the door of the school,
the principal said, “Good morning,
Amy. How are you today?”

“Wonderful,” said Amy.
“But I had strange dreams
last night.”

“I bet,” said the principal.

Then Amy walked into her classroom and everyone . . .

snored.

zzz-zzz-zzz-zzz

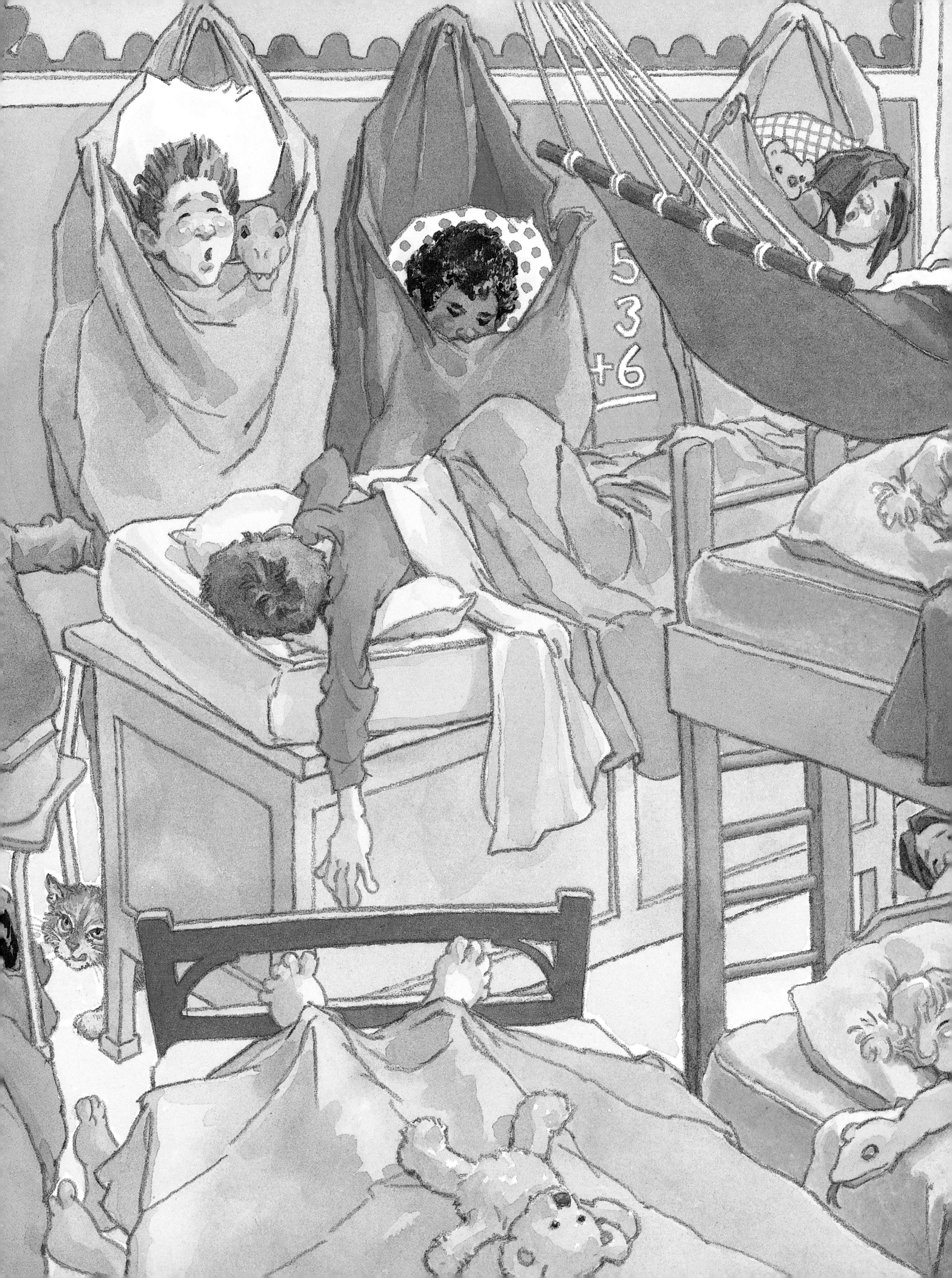
5
3
+6

About Get Out of Bed!

In 1995, Amy Albrecht's mother wrote me a letter about how hard it was to get Amy out of bed. She had even tried to wake Amy up by standing her on her feet, and Amy just fell over and went to sleep on the floor. One day Amy's mother said maybe she should take Amy to school in her bed! Amy thought that was a really funny idea and said that it would make a great Robert Munsch story. So Amy and her mother each wrote me a letter about it. I read the letters, wrote *Get Out of Bed!*, sent it back to Amy and then forgot about it. In 1998, my editor came across the story and said "Hey, Bob! Let's do this one."

After the book was done, Amy invited me to the Fall Fair in her hometown of Tavistock, Ontario. Her family had made a float for the parade. The float was Amy in her bed, with the bed on a hay wagon. I was sitting beside Amy reading her a book and lots of her friends were there in their pyjamas yelling "AMY! GET OUT OF BED!" Amy's float won first prize.

— R.M.

For Chris Duggan,
Guelph, Ontario.
—R.M.

Mmm, Cookies!

by Robert Munsch

illustrated by
Michael Martchenko

Christopher walked down into the basement and saw a big pile of play clay in the corner.

"Wow!" said Christopher. "I love play clay."

So he got himself a piece of red play clay and whapped it in his hands —
WHAP, WHAP, WHAP, WHAP, WHAP.

Made it nice and round —
SWISH, SWISH, SWISH, SWISH, SWISH.

Sprinkled it with sugar —
CHIK, CHIK, CHIK, CHIK, CHIK.

Covered it with yellow icing —
Glick, Glick, Glick, Glick, Glick.

And put some raisins on top —
PLUNK, PLUNK, PLUNK, PLUNK, PLUNK.

Then Christopher went upstairs and said, "Mommy, look! Daddy made you a cookie!"

"Ohhhhh!" said his mother. "That's so nice! I didn't even know he could cook."

So she picked up that cookie
and took a big bite.

SCRRUUUNNNNCH!

And she yelled, "YUCK!
PWAH! SPLICHT!
PLAY CLAY!
GLA-GLA-GLA-GLA!"

She ran to the bathroom and washed out her mouth for a long time —

SCRITCH-SCRITCH,
SCRITCH-SCRITCH,
SCRITCH-SCRITCH.

While his mother was washing out her mouth, Christopher got himself another piece of red play clay.

He whapped it in his hands —
WHAP, WHAP, WHAP, WHAP, WHAP.
Made it nice and round —
SWISH, SWISH, SWISH, SWISH, SWISH.
Sprinkled it with sugar —
CHIK, CHIK, CHIK, CHIK, CHIK.
Covered it with yellow icing —
Glick, Glick, Glick, Glick, Glick.
And put some raisins on top —
PLUNK, PLUNK, PLUNK, PLUNK, PLUNK.
Then he went upstairs to find his father.

Christopher said, “Daddy, look! Mommy made you a cookie.”

“Ohhhhh!” said his father. “That’s so nice! It’s been a long time since your mother made me cookies.”

So he picked it up and took a big bite.

SCRRUUUNNNNCH!

And he yelled, "YUCK!
PWAH! SPLICHT!
PLAY CLAY!
GLA-GLA-GLA-GLA!"

That cookie tasted so bad, he ran to the bathroom and washed out his mouth.

SCRITCH-SCRITCH,
SCRITCH-SCRITCH,
SCRITCH-SCRITCH.

By the time his father and mother came out of the bathroom, Christopher was late for school.

So they called up the teacher and said, "Christopher is giving people PLAY CLAY cookies!"

"Don't worry," said the teacher. "I know just what to do."

She got herself some red play clay and whapped it in her hands —
WHAP, WHAP, WHAP, WHAP, WHAP.

Made it nice and round —
SWISH, SWISH, SWISH, SWISH, SWISH.

Sprinkled it with sugar —
CHIK, CHIK, CHIK, CHIK, CHIK.

Covered it with yellow icing —
Glick, Glick, Glick, Glick, Glick.

And put some raisins on top —
PLUNK, PLUNK, PLUNK, PLUNK, PLUNK.

Then she put the cookie on Christopher's chair.

Aa Bb Cc Dd Ee Ff Gg Hh Ii Jj Kk

When Christopher came in, he said, “Look at the lovely cookie!” He picked it up and took a big bite.

SCRRUUUNNNNCH!

And he yelled, “YUCK!
PWAH! SPLICHT!
PLAY CLAY!
GLA-GLA-GLA-GLA!”

That cookie tasted so bad, he ran to the bathroom and washed out his mouth.

BURBLE
BURBLE SPLAT
SPLICHT
BWAHHH.

When Christopher came back from the bathroom, the teacher said, "And now would everyone like to make some REAL cookies?"

And the class yelled "YES!"

And when Christopher was done with his cookie . . .

he took it home to give to his
mother and father.

About Mmm, Cookies!

When I worked in daycare, I used to play a game with the kids. When they were at the play clay table, I would come over and say, "Has anybody made me a cookie today?" Each kid would then make me a play clay cookie and laugh when I tried to eat it. The kids NEVER got tired of it. Eventually, I made up a lot of different stories that all had me eating something yucky. The kids loved it when I made terrible noises because I had eaten something terrible.

All these stories sort of boiled down into this one story, and by 1985 it had stopped changing. I did not have a particular kid for the story, so when I decided it should be a book I went looking for a kid. I did not have to look far. On my street was Christopher, who delighted in freaking out big people. He happily volunteered to be the kid in the book. The crazy hair and wild-eyed look that Christopher has in the book are taken from photographs. He really did look like that when he was little.

It is fun to play around with the sound effects in this story and make them your own! You do not have to read them the way they are in the book. I often change them when I tell the story. Sometimes a kid will yell, "THAT'S WRONG! YOU DON'T KNOW YOUR OWN STORY!"

— R.M.

To Ali and Kate Lucas,
Goose Bay, Newfoundland and Labrador.
—R.M.

Deep Snow

by **Robert Munsch**
illustrated by **Michael Martchenko**

Way out in the middle of nowhere on the snowmobile, Ali suddenly yelled, "STOP!"

"What's the matter?" said her father.

"I want to jump in the snow," said Ali.

"No," said her sister Kate, "that is deep, deep, deeeeeeeep snow!"

"I still want to jump in it," said Ali.

"This is not a good idea," said Kate.

Ali stood up on the seat, gave her best yell, jumped out as far as she could, landed in the snow and disappeared. All that was left was a hole in the snow.

"She is totally gone," said Kate. "She's at the bottom of a drift."

"Kate," said their father, "jump down that hole and help Ali get out."

"This is also a bad idea," said Kate, but she jumped down the hole anyway.

For a long time nothing happened.

Then their father climbed off the snowmobile, crawled over to the hole in the snow and said, "Hey, Ali and Kate! How are you doing down there?"

Ali and Kate said, "Murfs farmble gulgph," because their mouths were full of snow.

Their father said, "Ali and Kate, speak clearly. I can't hear you."

Ali got the snow out of her mouth and yelled, "Get us out of here!"

"Don't worry," said their father. He reached down the hole as far as he could, got hold of something and pulled very hard.

Ali yelled, "That's my ear!"
So he let go of the ear, reached down the hole, got hold of something else and pulled very hard.
Kate yelled, "That's my nose!"

So he let go of the nose, reached down the hole as far as he could, got hold of something else and pulled very hard.
Ali yelled, "That's my lip!"

Finally he got hold of their ponytails, pulled as hard as he could, and Ali and Kate came flying out of the hole.
"Good," said their dad. "Now we can go."

"No, we can't," said Ali and Kate. "Our boots are still at the bottom of the hole."

"Oh, rats," said their father. He crawled over to the hole and reached down as far as he could. He didn't find their boots, so he reached way, way, way, way down and fell into the hole. Only his boots were sticking up out of the snow.

Ali crawled over to the boots and said, "Hey, Dad! How are you doing down there?"

Their father said, "Murfs farmble gulgph," because his mouth was full of snow.

"Speak clearly," said Kate. "We can't understand you."

"Murfs farmble gulgph," said their father, and then he got the snow out of his mouth and yelled, "GET ME OUT OF HERE!"

Ali and Kate took hold of their dad's feet and pulled as hard as they could. Nothing happened.

"This is very bad," said Ali. "Daddy will have to stay there till springtime. How can he fly his jet for the air force if he is stuck at the bottom of a hole?"

Then Kate got an idea. She ran over to the snowmobile and got a rope. She tied one end of the rope around their father's foot and tied the other end to the snowmobile. Then Ali and Kate jumped on the snowmobile and went down the trail as fast as they could.

Their father came flying up out of the hole and bounced down the trail after the snowmobile yelling,

"Ow ouch! Ow ouch! Ow ouch!
STOP! STOP! STOP! STOP!"

So Kate stopped the snowmobile and there was their father, lying in the snow.

"Daddy," said Ali, "You didn't get our boots after all. We're going to have to do it again."

"Right," said their father. "Let's do it again."

He tied a rope to Ali and Kate's feet and dropped them down the hole.

And he came by later to get them out.

OAKS

About Deep Snow

In 1991, I was on a storytelling trip in Labrador. My son, Andrew, was with me. In Goose Bay we stayed with Ali and Kate Lucas, whose dad was a Canadian Forces pilot. Andrew liked jet planes, and I thought, "Wow! I bet I am going to get a good jet plane story."

One afternoon we went for a walk on a snowmobile trail. Andrew and I did not know that the snow in the woods was very, very deep. Andrew thought it would be fun to jump off the trail, and he went way down into the snow. He loved it. Ali and Kate jumped in after him. They did not go that far down into the snow, but Kate got her foot stuck, so I went to help. I did not know that in some places the snow was covering whole pine trees and the trees made an empty place under the snow. So when I walked off the trail I fell through, way, way, way over my head. It took me a long time to climb back up, and Kate was still stuck! We finally got her out, but her boots were still at the bottom of the hole. Since I was already wet, I went head-first down into the hole to get her boots. While I was head-first in the snow with my feet sticking out, I started thinking of a story called "Deep Snow." So this is my only story that started while I was upside-down in the snow.

— R.M.

About Robert Munsch

Who is Robert Munsch? He's one of North America's best-loved storytellers, and his books, including the best-selling *Love You Forever,* have been entertaining children for decades.

Robert grew up in a family of nine kids. You might think that would be pretty hard, but he says it was a good thing. He could do the things he liked — like reading — without much interruption. When Robert was younger, he was a "reading freak" and would read anything he could. His favourite book was *The Five Hundred Hats of Bartholomew Cubbins* by Dr. Seuss. He also liked to write poems — funny ones, of course.

It might be hard to believe, but Robert wasn't always a writer. He was working at a daycare centre when his boss's wife, a children's librarian, heard him telling stories. She thought the stories were very good, and told him he should write them down and send them to a publisher.

Can you imagine: nine publishers turned down his stories! Finally one publisher said yes, and that very first Robert Munsch book, *Mud Puddle*, came out in 1979. Even so, it was another five years before Robert finally quit his job at the daycare centre. Since then he has published more than forty books!

Where does Robert get his ideas? They almost always come from kids. Sometimes he'll see someone in the audience when he is doing a storytelling and ask if they would like to be a character in one of the stories. Other times, he'll be inspired by a kid he meets or by a letter someone sends to him. Just about anything can give him an idea. But not all of his stories become books — there are just too many! When he does a storytelling session, he might tell fourteen or fifteen stories, most of them new. But sometimes one story seems stronger than the rest, so he'll take that one and tell it over and over again — sometimes for years. And one day he might decide that the story is ready to become a book.

It's important to Robert that his books can be enjoyed by kids regardless of where they live in North America, or even the world. So if a story is set in Toronto, he wants kids in the Northwest Territories to enjoy it just as much as ones who live in the city, and vice versa. It can be a real trick to get the stories to work out so kids everywhere can relate to them.

Robert likes telling stories in schools and libraries. Sometimes, if he's going to be in a particular area, he'll check to see if a local school has written to him. Then he'll pay them a surprise visit. Sometimes he'll call a library or school and ask them to find an interesting family that he can stay with when he is travelling. Lucky them!

What does Robert do for fun? He likes to read, take his dogs for walks outside of town, ride his bicycle and even climb trees! And he loves to eat "hot, hot chicken wings."

Robert has three children, Julie, Andrew and Tyya, and he's written stories for all of them. The family in *Andrew's Loose Tooth* is Robert Munsch's — or Michael Martchenko's version of them, anyway.

Robert also keeps busy by reading and responding to the letters he gets. Each month he gets about 200 letters from schools and another 200 from individual children. That's a lot of reading and writing to catch up on!

Being a good storyteller is something that Robert has been blessed with. Still, it took him a long time to realize that he was pretty good at it. He often wonders exactly what it is that makes a person a great storyteller. Being able to think on your feet is part of it, but it's also really important to be a good listener — especially when it comes to listening to children. Of course, he's so good at telling stories that it's made him popular with children the world over.

Being a writer takes dedication as well as talent, but as Robert says, "This is the best job I've ever had."

About Michael Martchenko

Michael Martchenko's art is well known to kids, parents and teachers across the country — and although he's illustrated books by lots of writers (including himself!), he is best known for his work with Robert Munsch.

Michael has always loved drawing. As a boy, he copied comic book covers, imitating the lines and colour. "It was great practice," he says. He was unable to take art classes in high school, but that didn't stop him. He still knew he wanted to be an artist, so he decided to study illustration at the Ontario College of Art in Toronto.

After graduating, Michael worked as a junior art director for an advertising company. His job was to work on storyboards, designing ads. That's where he thought he'd stay for the rest of his life. Then one day, at an art show, Robert saw Michael's work and was attracted to his lively style. He approached Michael to do the pictures for *The Paper Bag Princess*, and a terrific partnership was born.

At first, Michael didn't think much of the story. "My first reaction was 'Yuck!'" he says. He thought it was a typical fairy tale about a prince and princess. But then he read it and thought, "This is cool!"

But Michael didn't quit his advertising job at first. "I thought illustrating books was something I could do when I retired," he says. "I never thought about doing it full-time." So he would work during the day at the advertising agency, then spend the evenings and weekends working on his picture book illustrations.

Michael has now been creating picture books full-time for about ten years, and he couldn't be happier. "I love what I do," he says.

What's his secret to illustrating? When he first gets a story, Michael doesn't draw the sketches right away. Instead, he'll get what he calls "mind pictures" of what would work in the story. Then he'll do thumbnail sketches, or storyboards, just like he did when he was an art director. Full pencil drawings come next. Then the paintings are done in watercolours.

And what about the funny background images that his fans love? Well, he didn't always do them. As time went on, the ideas started to come to him. He didn't set out to have, say, a monkey helping other animals escape from the zoo, as in *Alligator Baby*. "They just happen," he says of the extra touches. Readers have come to expect them, but he believes that it's important to make sure that those background images aren't too distracting.

When he was doing the illustrations for *Mmm, Cookies!*, Michael started what has become a tradition in his books with Robert Munsch — he put in a pterodactyl. Robert liked it so much, he asked Michael to put it in all their books, and that's just what Michael does. (Look for it in *Deep Snow*, the special bonus story in this book.)

What does Michael like to do besides illustrate? He loves history and airplanes. In fact, he collects aviation material, like old uniforms and badges. He's created paintings of historical planes. He also recently picked up his guitar again. This helps him to relax a little from his busy schedule.

Michael Martchenko and Robert Munsch have developed a wonderful partnership, and their collaboration has brought great happiness to many people over the years. And, just as important, Michael has found great happiness himself.

"I still can't believe I'm doing this for a living," he says.

About Alan and Lea Daniel

Alan and Lea Daniel are the perfect example of a successful team. As artists, they help each other bring the vision of writers like Robert Munsch to life. They also have a wonderful family, including three children and three grandchildren.

At first, Alan illustrated alone. But once Alan and Lea's youngest child started school, Lea, who had always loved to paint, began to help Alan with his busy work schedule. This partnership has lasted throughout the years, with Lea and Alan working together to create the colourful illustrations that they're known for.

Lea says that one of the funniest things about working with Alan is that he'll often act out what he's drawing. So if a character is happy, you'll see Alan's face break into a smile, and if the character is puzzled, you'll see his brow start to furrow.

How do Alan and Lea get the ideas for their pictures? They often look for the humour in the stories they work on. In the case of *Get Out of Bed!*, they really enjoyed Robert Munsch's wacky sense of fun. They had a great time adding various pets for Amy — and if you look closely at the illustrations, you'll find even more of their funny touches, like characters from other stories.

Alan and Lea also like to take people and things from their lives and add them to their illustrations. So sometimes a child in their neighbourhood may be the basis for a character in a book, or, as in *Get Out of Bed!*, one of their dogs may become one of the character's many pets. Readers may not recognize these personal details, but they help make each book special for this artistic team.

About Eugenie Fernandes

Eugenie Fernandes was probably born to be an artist. Almost everybody in her family is involved with art in some way. Her father was one of the very first comic book illustrators, and Eugenie's husband and both her children are artists too.

When Eugenie was approached to illustrate *Ribbon Rescue*, she jumped at the chance. "Who wouldn't want to illustrate a Robert Munsch book?" she laughs. She says that she finds all of Robert's books to be full of energy, and it's this energy that she tried to bring to her illustrations.

For *Ribbon Rescue*, Robert Munsch brought her pictures of Jillian, the girl on whom the story is based, along with photos of her family and her community. Eugenie was able to take them and add her own special touches to help bring the story to life for readers.

Eugenie insists that to be successful at anything in life, you need to be persistent. "If you have to be an artist," she says, "you have to be an artist." She spent years taking different illustrating jobs before she could do it full-time. "You can't give up," she says.

What would Eugenie have done if she hadn't become an artist? She might have studied biology, like her mother, and done something with animals or plants. Even now, some of her favourite things to draw are starfish, seashells, flowers, and leaves.

Eugenie continues to illustrate and write her own stories. And when she's not in her studio, overlooking a lake in eastern Ontario, she can be found watching the sunrise or taking a walk along the shore. Perhaps that's where she finds the inspiration for the special touches she adds to her illustrations — like the frogs that hop all through *Ribbon Rescue*!